The world has waited so long for you, little one.

Your story is just beginning, and there are so many wonderful chapters ahead.

Even before
you arrived you
were wished
for, longed for
and so loved.

Everyone was so excited to hear about you!

Now our world is a better place with you in it.

Everyone is delighted at your arrival.

You are going on an amazing journey.

You have so many wonderful moments ahead of you,

there is so much to look forward to as you grow.

There are a few things for you to remember along the way . . .

The world is full of surprises, waiting just for you! Every day brings new adventures and wonders to explore.

With each one,

you'll grow in your own special way.

Cherish the people you meet who see your spark and fill your heart with joy.

When you work hard and never give up, your dreams can come true.

Every step you take will bring you closer to all you hope to be.

Be kind to others.
Your kindness will
make the world even
more beautiful.

The love you give to others will return to you.

Love, shared, is the greatest gift of all.

Most importantly, always . . .

The World Waited For You first published by **FROM YOU TO ME LTD** in 2025.

For a full range of our titles where gifts can also be personalised, please visit

WWW.FROMYOUTOME.COM

FROM YOU TO ME are committed to a sustainable future for our business, our customers and our planet. This book was printed and bound in Shenzhen, China in January 2026 on FSC® certified paper.

This book is EUDR compliant.

All rights reserved. No part of this publication may be reproduced, stored in a retrieval system, or transmitted in any form or by any means electronic, mechanical, photocopying, recording, or otherwise, without the prior written permission of the copyright owner who can be contacted via the publisher at the above website address.

3 5 7 9 11 12 10 8 6 4

Copyright © 2025 **FROM YOU TO ME LTD**

ISBN 978-1-907048-98-2

Written and illustrated by Lucy Tapper & Steve Wilson fromlucy.com.

FROM YOU TO ME LTD, STUDIO 100, THE OLD LEATHER FACTORY
GLOVE FACTORY STUDIOS, HOLT, WILTSHIRE, BA14 6RJ, UK